Cheeky Charlie

Mat Waugh

Cheeky Charlie

Mat Waugh

This book is for sale at
http://leanpub.com/cheekycharlie

This version was published on 2015-03-20

ISBN 978-1508910510

Leanpub

This is a Leanpub book. Leanpub empowers authors
and publishers with the Lean Publishing process.

For D, I and K. I'll never have a more adoring (or fidgety) audience.

With gratitude also to the late Dorothy Edwards – without her Naughty Little Sister, we wouldn't have Charlie.

Note for grown-ups: *If you're reading this book to smaller children – the sort who think that clowns' noses really do honk when you squeeze them – you might want to give the 'Christmas Fair' chapter a skim read first. It contains a minor spoiler, though Saint Nick himself emerges unscathed.*

Contents

Stuff you need to know

Hello. My name is Harry. I'm 6 years old, but I'm very nearly 7. I'm quite clever, and quite pretty, I think: I can tell the time and my hair is long and wavy, although it sometimes gets quite tangly. It's hard to describe the colour, although my Daddy says it's like straw in the morning and honey in the evening, which is half-rude and half-nice. That's normal for Daddy.

When the sun shines, I get freckles on my nose. When I was little I didn't like them. I stood on the chair in the bathroom so that I could see myself in the mirror. Then I rubbed them really hard with a flannel until my face was red and sore. I thought I'd got rid of them for a while, but then my face stopped being red and they came back. Mummy came in and found me crying.

"What's the matter Harry?" she asked.

"I've got spots," I sobbed, and pointed to my nose. My cousin Freya complains about her spots whenever she comes for a sleepover, although I can never see them.

Mummy smiled then, which I didn't think was very

nice because I was upset, but then she gave me a cuddle, which felt better. "They're not spots, they're summer sprinkles," she said, "and they make you look gorgeous."

And then I started to think about sprinkles: sprinkles on cakes, sprinkles on fairies, even about the water sprinkler we sometimes play with in the garden. And I decided that having sprinkles on your face is a good thing.

I've just had a thought. You do know I'm a girl, don't you? People are always getting it wrong, and it makes me quite cross. In fact my uncle Mike calls me "Prince Harry" just to annoy me. He tells me to thump him really hard if I don't like it so I do, right in his tummy. But he just laughs until I jump on him and scream at him to stop.

My real name is actually Harriet, but everyone calls me Harry. Mummy says that I could call myself Hattie if I wanted, but I think that sounds silly, so I don't.

Actually not everyone calls me Harry; Granny always calls me Harriet. Whenever anyone talks about my name, she shakes her head so that her curly white hair wobbles, and she makes a funny sucking noise. There's a funny story I want to tell you about Granny, but Mummy has just reminded me that this book is supposed to be about Charlie, my little brother. So let me tell you about him straight away.

Do you have a little brother? Mummy says you might have, but I bet he's not like Charlie. So I need to explain.

Do you have a board at school where they put WOW words? You know, the interesting words that the teachers say you should use in your stories instead of 'nice'? We do. And sometimes I imagine that Charlie has rubbed himself all over with a glue stick and then rolled along that board, covering himself in WOW words. Because lots of them are perfect to describe Charlie. Are you ready?

Here are the ones I wrote down:

- irritating
- exuberant
- energetic
- astonishing
- insolent
- mischievous
- cunning
- filthy
- affectionate
- odorous

There's lots more, I'll copy some more down and tell you.

But there is another way to describe him, and you know it already because it's what I've decided to call this book: Cheeky Charlie. That's what Daddy calls Charlie all the time: when he's shouted something rude, when he's done something naughty, when he wants him to budge up on the sofa. And most times he ruffles Charlie's hair when he says it, too.

He tried that once with me and I went crazy. He said, "Alright Hattie, keep your hair on," and that made Mummy laugh really loud which made me even angrier. So I stomped upstairs and played on his iPad without telling him, just to teach him a lesson.

But Charlie really is very cheeky, and that's what my book is about: all the naughty things that Charlie has done. My teachers say that it's not nice to tell tales, but you don't know Charlie, so you can't get him told off.

But if you ever meet my Mummy, you mustn't tell her what I tell you about Charlie, because then *I'll* get into trouble. Do you promise? Proper promise? Pinky promise?

Brilliant, because I've got loads to tell you. Some of it happened ages ago, some of it happened just last week. Some of it is funny, some of it is a bit sad, and lots of it is disgusting, because that's what Charlie can be. It might even make you be sick, so get ready.

*   *   *

I once asked Daddy to tell me about the naughtiest thing he had ever done.

"Not much to choose from," he said. "I was an angel. I always worked hard, did my homework on time, tidied my bedroom, went to bed early, got up late. Not like your mother, she was a really wild child."

I looked at Mummy who was sitting on the sofa, making her eyes roll around in her head, and pulling a funny face.

"Don't believe him, Harry," said Mummy. "He ate his brother's birthday cake. He once vomited on the dog. He almost crashed your Grandad's car. Your Dad was a right handful."

"Handful of what?" I asked.

"Trouble," said Mummy.

Next door, where Charlie was watching telly, there was a crash.

"Charlie? Are you OK?" shouted Mummy, getting up off the sofa.

"Yes Mummy!" shouted Charlie. "I just falled off the table."

"Fell, Charlie, not falled," shouted Mummy back. "OK, just be careful," she said, sitting back down again. "Now you know where Charlie gets it from."

"Are you talking about my little Charlie?" said Daddy. "He's a goodie two-shoes like me. Although I wouldn't let him drive my car. Or leave him on his own with a dog. Or my birthday cake, come to think of it."

"That would be OK," I said. "All the candles would scare him away."

"Oi!" said Daddy, and he threw a cushion at me. It bounced off my arm, onto the table and nearly knocked Mummy's mug of tea over, the one with 'Top Teacher' written on it.

Mummy looked at Daddy, and raised her eyebrows, making her forehead all wrinkly.

"Harry's arm was in the wrong place," mumbled Dad. "Not my fault."

Look, I haven't got long today, because I'm going for a haircut soon, and I always get a lolly so I don't want to miss it. But come back, and I'll start to tell you lots of stories about what Charlie has done. And they're a lot, lot worse than you think.

Felt tips

The first story I'm going to tell you about Charlie is one that I told at school last term in front of the whole class. Mrs Schofield had asked if anyone "had been up to anything interesting" during the holidays.

After I'd finished, Mrs Schofield said, "You told that well, Harry, but it was supposed to be a true story."

"But it was a true story!" I protested. "I can show you the photo..." But wait a minute. I almost told you the ending and spoiled it.

So let's go back to the beginning. Mummy and Daddy decided that their bedroom was too small and that they didn't want to share a bathroom with us any more, because children wee on toilet seats. That's true. Sometimes the toilets at school have buckets of wee on them.

So Mummy and Daddy asked Jim from down the road to help. Jim is a builder. He has crazy curly ginger hair and a very big belly. He wears really old, tight t-shirts that have started to go see-through. Sometimes you can see his belly button through them, and it looks like someone's pushed their finger into a balloon.

He drives an ancient white van, and that has see-through bits and funny stains on it, too. In the seat next to him there are two other men who work with him, but they're never the same. Maybe they don't like his t-shirts.

So Jim came round to look at our house. He stood outside, pointing at windows and walls, scribbling on a dirty piece of paper, and then he went away again. I forgot all about him until one sunny morning, when he walked past the kitchen window while I was eating my breakfast.

"Mummy, Jim is in our garden!" I shouted.

"What?" she said, and went outside. I watched her talk to him, and then she came back in, shaking her head.

"What does he want?" I asked.

"He's starting the building work today," Mummy said, "we just weren't expecting him, that's all."

And that's how it began. Jim started bringing spades and pick axes and toolboxes and even an orange cement mixer down the side passage, helped by two men I hadn't seen before. One wore a blue tracksuit and the other wore a red tracksuit, and Red Tracksuit stared right at me as he walked past. I ducked down in front of the washing machine.

When I felt brave enough to take another look, I got an

even bigger shock. Red and Blue had both taken their tops off, and were now digging up the patio. I was just about to shout for Mummy when Charlie came in, and pressed his nose against the back door.

"Who that?" he asked, pointing at Red. "What's he doing? Why has someone done a drawing on him?" he continued.

Charlie asks a lot of questions. And sure enough, Red had a tattoo of a lady on his back – a lady with no clothes on.

Mummy came in then, and took Charlie out to meet Red and Blue and Jim. I stayed inside and watched, as Charlie went straight up to Red and pointed at his tattoo. Everybody laughed, and Jim picked Charlie up so he could touch it. He traced the outline of the lady with his finger, while Red pretended that he was being tickled. Everyone laughed again.

Over the next few days the holes in the garden got bigger and bigger, and the piles of earth and clay got higher and higher. Eventually you could only see Red and Blue's sweaty faces as they worked – Jim never seemed to be around. They put planks of wood across the trenches so that we could get to the trampoline and the garden shed. Every day, whenever Red and Blue stopped for a cup of tea, Charlie would go up behind Red and run his finger over his tattoo. Red soon stopped pretending to laugh, but he didn't seem to mind.

I was in the kitchen, helping Mummy make pizzas. It was another hot day – 'sweltering', Mrs Schofield says – and Red and Blue were digging again. Charlie was pulling Mummy's apron.

"Hungry, Mummy! Me hungry Mummy!" he said.

"You could have an apple," she said.

"Don't want a napple," said Charlie.

"Or an orange?"

"Don't want a norange," said Charlie.

"Or a banana?"

"Don't want a nana," said Charlie.

"Well there's nothing else for you to eat," said Mummy, "especially when you're being so rude. Go out and play until lunch is ready."

Charlie toddled off through the open back door and went straight up to Red and Blue. They were sitting with their legs dangling into a hole, eating their lunch in the sunshine.

"Why are you digging? Have you found any treasure? Why have you stopped? Are you tired? Are you stronger than Daddy? What's in your sandwiches? They smell yucky," we heard him burble.

Red didn't reply. He just turned away from Charlie and shook his head. Charlie wrinkled his nose, which he does when he doesn't get what he wants, and stomped off to his den behind the shed. Meanwhile Blue drove away in the van, and Red stretched out on his tummy on the grass, and closed his eyes.

"Serves Charlie right," said Mummy, watching through the window, and we started to put the pizza toppings on. Ham first, then cheese, but never mushrooms. Do you like mushrooms? I don't, I think they're weird.

Charlie reappeared.

"Mummy, where are my felt tips?"

"In the living room," said Mummy, "but take your shoes off first!"

I wondered why he wanted felt tips. Mummy didn't normally allow Charlie to use them on his own, because once he drew smiley faces on the wall up the stairs. He must've sat on each step and got lots of practice, because by the top they were really quite good. Daddy went loopy crazy. "But I did eyebrows and lots of colours!" Charlie had said, though for once it didn't get him out of trouble.

Anyway, Charlie took the whole pot of felt tips back

out into the garden, crossed the plank, and sat down next to the sleeping Red. He thought for a bit, and chose a green felt tip. Slowly, carefully, he got to work.

Now normally, when Charlie is naughty, I never see it happen. I don't know why, he's like a secret little spy who does stuff when you're not looking. But this time I saw everything. And because Red was a grumpy man, I didn't tell anyone. I just let him do it.

A little while later Charlie and I were playing in the lounge when we heard someone laughing very hard indeed, and another man shouting. I couldn't understand the shouter, but he didn't sound happy. Charlie looked at me in a funny way – a little bit pleased, a little bit frightened.

Mummy came downstairs to see what was happening, and we went with her into the kitchen.

Beyond, in the garden, Blue was crouching down on the grass. At first I thought he was hurt, because tears were streaming down his cheeks, but then I realised that he was the one who was laughing loudly. Red was standing up, doing that twisty-turny thing where you try to look at your own back, and all the time he was shouting at the top of his voice.

"Do you know what's going on, Harry?" said Mummy.

"It wasn't me," I said. "I didn't do anything."

"Hmm," said Mummy, "that's not what I asked. Charlie, any ideas?"

"Nuffink," he said. "I done nuffink."

He didn't look like he'd done nuffink though. He looked like he'd definitely done somefink – and I knew what it was.

Mum was at the door, and blocked our way.

"I think it's best if you stay inside – especially you, Charlie," she said.

He swivelled round, and we now could see what Red was shouting about. The naked lady on his back... well she wasn't naked any more. She now wore a pair of bright green trousers, and a purple and brown stripy top. And an orange hat. And she was carrying a blue handbag.

Charlie had obviously thought that her face needed work, too, because he had given her some big goggly eyes, a small beard, and big ears like an elephant.

To complete the scene there were some wobbly clouds on Red's shoulders, and a large sun on Red's shoulder, drawn in thick black pen.

"A black sun? Couldn't you find your yellow felt tip?" asked Mummy, and we looked up to see Mummy rubbing her eyes. "Oh dear oh dear, Charlie, what have you done this time?" she said, laughing.

Now I think you'd agree that drawing on somebody is pretty naughty. I was sure that Charlie was in the biggest trouble of his life. But something strange happened.

When Daddy got home, Mummy showed him Red's back – she'd taken a photo on her phone so he could see what it looked like. And instead of going mad, Daddy roared with laughter, just like Blue had. He couldn't stop. He grabbed Charlie, shouting "Come here my little doodle bug!" and they fell onto the sofa, laughing like crazy.

"That's your best yet," said Daddy in between chuckles. "You made her look like the elephant man."

"She's not a man she's a lady!" protested Charlie. "And I did a big smile on her!"

"I know you did," said Daddy, holding Charlie upside down and swinging him from side to side, "and you didn't colour over the lines. You're a proper little artist, Cheeky Charlie!"

Treasure

Not long after the felt tips incident, Charlie was in trouble again. Big trouble. And this time Daddy wasn't laughing one little bit.

You need to know that Charlie had become obsessed with pirates. He had books about pirates, DVDs about pirates, even a scratchy pirate costume with an eye patch that he wore to school.

He even talked like a pirate. "More cornflakes, pea hearties!" he'd shout at breakfast.

"Yo ho ho and a bottle of yum!" he'd yell at lunch.

"I'm burying the treasure!" he'd declare at dinner, when Mummy caught him trying to push his peas under the baked potato skins.

The sun that had been shining when Charlie did his colouring in on Red's back had gone. Day after day the rain tipped down, filling the builders' holes with brown, muddy water.

To Charlie, this was just another pirate adventure waiting to happen. As soon as the rain stopped and Mummy opened the back door, Charlie rushed into the garden.

"I'm off to find the treasure!" he shouted, with his slightly-too-big pirate hat sliding off his head. "Come on Harry, let's find the treasure!"

"No thanks," I said. "It's wet, cold and muddy, and there's no treasure in our garden."

But he wasn't listening. "Pirate Charlie cross the bang plank!" I heard him shout as he wobbled his way across the trenches and rushed off up the garden, waving his toy spade.

I went inside to watch CBBC – Tracy Beaker was just starting. I love Tracy Beaker. A few minutes later I heard Mummy shout in the kitchen.

"Charlie, just look at the state of you! What on earth have you been doing?" Charlie mumbled something I couldn't hear.

"But that's not treasure, darling, it's an old flowerpot."

I laughed. Boys can be so stupid.

"And that's a bit of glass, you shouldn't even be playing with that...and that's – hang on, what is that?" said Mummy. "Let's give it a wash and see."

That sounded more interesting. I walked through to the kitchen, where Charlie was standing on the stool at the sink. His arms were crusted with brown mud; his shorts were wet right through, and he had a big smear of mud on his face, too – probably because he'd been picking his nose.

"What's that, Mummy?" I asked. "Is it money?"

"It's my treasure," said Charlie, pulling a face.

Mummy was holding a big brown coin, rubbing it and peering at it closely.

"Hey Charlie, you're right, it is treasure. It's an old penny!"

"What, one penny?" I said. "Just 1p?"

"Yes, but it's nearly 80 years old," replied Mummy. "Charlie, that's brilliant. Well done!"

"Wow Charlie that's amaaazing," I added. "You've found 1p, you're so clever. I've got 80p in my piggy bank."

"If you can't say anything nice, Harry, then don't bother," said Mummy.

I went back to watch Tracy Beaker, pulling the door shut behind me.

That evening, Daddy made a massive fuss of my brother, telling him he was a tip-top pirate and an expert treasure finder, and rolled around on the carpet with him while they both shouted "Ha haaaar!"

I couldn't stand it.

"Shush!" I shouted. "I can't hear the telly!"

"Oooh," said Daddy, "one of the crew is revolting! Shall we throw her overboard?"

He tried to grab me, but I was too quick, and ran out of the room. He can be so annoying sometimes!

*   *   *

The next day, Charlie rushed out into the garden after breakfast. The builders still weren't back, so he had the whole muddy place to himself. Very soon his pirate outfit was ruined, his hat had fallen into a puddle and he'd lost his eyepatch. He won't be wearing that again for World Book Day.

But the hunt went on, and he poked around with his spade in every nook and cranny, muttering "Pea hearties" to himself.

More than once, he ran in excitedly to show Mummy his loot.

"That's a bottle top," said Mummy the first time.

"That's an old piece of string," said Mummy when he reappeared. "Not sure we'll get much for that."

"That's... ugh, Charlie, what is that? It stinks!" she said the next time, taking the dirty white object out of Charlie's grip. "Oh Charlie, that's an old chicken bone or something. It was probably left by a fox."

"Not a chicken bone, it's a dinosaur," said Charlie. "From a pirate dinosaur. Rrrarrgh."

"You may be right, Charlie Richards, but that disgusting thing is not staying in this house a moment longer," said Mummy, and she threw it in the bin. "It's time to come in and get yourself cleaned up."

*   *   *

That afternoon I played in my room while Charlie stomped all over the house. Sometimes I'd hear Mummy shout for him, and every time he'd be in a different room. I ignored him, especially when he wanted someone to wipe his bottom. Yuck.

After Daddy got home, Charlie sneaked back into the garden again, but he was back suspiciously quickly.

"I finded more treasure!" he declared.

"What've you got there, little fella?" said Daddy.

Charlie opened up his grubby fist to reveal a not-very-dirty medal, still with the ribbon attached. I recognised it straight away.

"That's Grandad's!" I said. "You're not supposed to touch those, is he Daddy?" I said.

"You're spot-on there Harry," said Daddy. Mummy, who was watching, disappeared into the hall without a word.

"Have you been rummaging in our bedroom, Charlie?"

Charlie stood there, his head hanging down, saying nothing.

"Charlie? This is serious. Tell Daddy what you've been up to."

I don't know why Daddy was asking: it was obvious. Charlie had taken Grandad's medal and pretended to find it in the garden. It actually belonged to Daddy's Grandad, who got it when he won an aeroplane fight in a war. He's dead now, which is why we have it, along with two other medals he won in other fights.

Mummy was standing at the door, holding Grandad's blue medal case. She opened it up and showed it to Daddy. Empty.

"OK Charlie, let's go. You need to show me where the medals are."

"Can I look?" I asked.

"No, you stay here," said Daddy. "I'm sure we'll be back in five minutes, won't we Charlie?"

Charlie didn't look sure at all, but they put on their wellies and went out into the garden, which by now was almost dark. I watched them walk up and down, with Daddy pointing at holes and piles of mud, and Charlie plodding along, looking down at the ground.

They weren't back in five minutes. They weren't back in ten minutes, and by then I was in my spotty bedtime onesie, and brushing my teeth.

"No joy," said Daddy as they came back in. "Guess I know what I'm doing tomorrow," he said.

*   *   *

And so next morning, Daddy was out in the garden with a spade, looking. At first Charlie was with him, poking at the soil with a garden cane. I watched from the doorway.

"Maybe I put it here," he said. "Or here. Or here. Or..."

"That's enough, Charlie," said Daddy. "Time to go in, please."

"But I..."

"No. Inside. *Now.*"

When Daddy uses that voice, even Charlie knows it's serious.

Daddy hadn't been out there very long when we heard him shout "Bingo!"

Through the window we saw him grinning, holding up a medal. "One more to find," he shouted, and picked up his spade.

But the last one didn't want to be found. He was out there while we went swimming. He was out there until Mummy called him in for lunch. And he went out again afterwards.

I found him later at the kitchen table, drinking tea.

"What you been doing Daddy?" said Charlie.

"Looking for Grandad's medal, silly," I said. "Did you find it, Daddy?" I asked.

"Nope," he said. "Not a sniff."

Charlie sniffed, loudly, and started to laugh. But it didn't last long, because Mummy gave him one of those strict looks, the ones that mean you're not doing the right thing.

"I wonder if there's another way," said Mummy.

"How's that then?" said Daddy. "Get a big digger in?"

"Not exactly," said Mummy. "Didn't Alan say he used to go metal detecting?"

Slowly, Daddy put down his tea. "You're right," he said. "You're a genius. I'll call him now." And he went to find his phone.

Alan is one of our neighbours. He lives with his wife, Sheila, and they are always in their front garden when I walk to school, planting flowers or mowing the lawn. Alan has a taxi, but it's not one of the black ones, it's just a white car.

Alan came round, and brought his metal detector. Have you seen one? They look a bit rubbish: like a plate on the end of a stick. You put these headphones on and wave the stick around, and it helps you to find stuff underground.

"Thanks for coming, Alan," said Daddy. "I couldn't live with myself if we lost his Aircrew medal."

"Aye, that's a good'un," said Alan.

Walking past Alan and Sheila's house, I once asked Mummy why Alan says "I" instead of "yes". But I must have said it too loud, because Alan smiled, put down his trowel, and told me that's how they talk where he comes from, in "God's own country".

"God's country? What, heaven?" I asked. "Have you been dead?"

"I come from Yorkshire, and it *is* a lot like heaven," said Alan, "only it's a bit handier for the motorway."

I had no idea what he was talking about.

"I'm from up north, where the savages live," he said. "And where the people say gr-ass instead of gr-arse."

Now then. Mary rode on an ass in the Bible, I know that because they told us at school. An ass is a type of donkey. Arse is a rude word for bottom. Why was Alan talking about donkeys and grass and bottoms? I gave up trying to understand.

Anyway, now Alan was in our kitchen, and very soon he was out in our garden with his headphones on. I wondered if he was listening to Taylor Swift. She's my favourite.

Just like Daddy, he was out there for ages. Charlie and I sat on the step, watching him. As I was getting bored, he bent down, dug about a bit with a spade, and picked something up.

It didn't look like a medal. It looked like a bit of old shoe.

"It's probably from a fox," I shouted. "We have loads of them."

"Not this one, lassie," said Alan. "Give your Dad a shout, will you?"

I fetched Daddy while Alan kicked off his muddy wellies and came into the kitchen.

"Have you found it, fella?" asked Daddy.

"Can't say that I have," said Alan, "but it's still worth a gander."

Here we go again. A gander is a boy goose, Mrs Schofield told us that. But if this dirty thing was worth a gander, how much is that? One pound? Twenty pounds? I've never tried to buy a goose, have you? Maybe this was Alan being a bit crazy again.

Daddy and Mummy gathered around, while Charlie and I stood on chairs for a better look.

The dirty object he'd found was a bag. Alan used his thumbs to push bits of soil off it, and unpicked a piece of cord that tied it closed.

He tipped the bag, and a handful of coins slid out onto the table.

"TREASURE!" shouted Charlie.

"Easy there flower," said Alan. "Let's see what we've got."

"Penny...1914," he said, peering at the first coin. "Another penny...1922. They're all pennies," he said.

I counted quickly. One, two, three... "Nine pennies!" I said. "That's not even enough for a finger of fudge!"

"Steady on now, lass," said Alan. "Some of these are worth a pretty penny, so to speak, or at least I think so. We've got some here from Queen Victoria, and a couple older than that. I think you could be looking at a few quid, Tom."

"Well well," said Daddy. "Can't say I'm happy about the medal, but this is a bit of a result, isn't it, gang?"

*   *   *

Later, after Alan had left carrying his metal detector and a pack of beer that Daddy had given him to say thanks, we all looked at the coins again, and Daddy gave them a wipe with a cloth.

It seemed amazing that these old pennies could be worth a lot of money.

"Where are we going to keep them?" asked Mummy. "That leather bag is falling apart. We need to put them somewhere out of harm's way," she said, looking at Charlie.

"Stick 'em into the medal case for now," said Daddy. "They'll fit where that missing one should go."

Mummy opened the medal case. She frowned, and looked a little more closely. I leaned over. There, sticking out between the case and the shiny blue medal holder inside, was a small piece of black, blue and yellow ribbon.

Mummy used her fingernail to hook it out from behind the holder. Attached to the ribbon was Grandad's missing star medal. Mummy swung it gently from her finger until Daddy noticed.

"You have *got* to be kidding me," he said. He walked up behind Charlie, and put his arms around him.

"Looks like the booty was right under our noses all along. And we found a little bit more along the way, didn't we Charlie? Maybe I won't throw you to the sharks just yet, Master Richards."

Aeroplane

Last summer, we went on an aeroplane. I'd been on an aeroplane loads of times before of course, but for Charlie it was his first time. "Airlane Airlane!" he kept shouting at breakfast, until Mummy told him to shhh and eat his Cheerios.

All the way to the airport Charlie wriggled and shuffled and shouted and moaned until even Daddy said that if Charlie didn't shut up, we'd turn round and go home again. I knew he didn't mean it – he says that all the time – and maybe Charlie knew it too, because he started blowing raspberries. We all ignored him and I looked out of the window.

The airport was busier than the supermarket after school. There were grown ups everywhere, but none of them looked happy about going on holiday. Children were running around, riding on suitcases and lying on trollies. Mummy held on to the back of our jumpers and pulled us close.

We joined the back of a big queue that wriggled like a lumpy, grumpy snake towards desk number 68. In front of us were a fat woman and a skinny man. The fat woman was sitting on a little wheelie suitcase.

Her bottom curved down on both sides until it was nearly touching the floor. The case was squished and the zip was coming undone, and a piece of red cloth was sticking out.

It reminded me of Magic Melvyn, the magician at my last birthday party. He had pulled a red hanky out of Charlie's ear, but Charlie doesn't like surprises so he turned round and thumped Magic right in the willy. Daddy says that's the naughtiest thing you can do. Magic went really red then, just like his hanky, and Daddy shouted so loud that some of my friends started crying, too.

But I was telling you about our trip on the aeroplane. In front of us, the skinny man took some money from the woman, and walked off towards the shops.

"Fatty bum bum!" shouted Charlie then, pointing. "Fatty fatty bummy bummy!" he said. He wasn't very good at talking, and he used to do that a lot. The woman didn't turn round, but she moved her head a bit and I could tell she was listening.

"Shh!" said Mummy, "That's a very rude thing to say to *me*, Charlie. We don't say things like that, it's not kind or polite."

"But Mummy," I said, "he didn't mean you, he meant -"

"No he definitely meant me, Harry," interrupted Mummy. "Now isn't that's a nice rabbit!" she went on, pointing at the picture I was drawing on her iPad.

She turned to Charlie. "Just wait nicely, and you can have some crisps on the plane."

"Cripps cripps cripps!" said Charlie, and he plonked his bottom on the floor. I told you he was a rude boy.

I tried to ignore him. I sat down on our trolley. I was just trying to get the ears right on my rabbit when I heard a very loud, very angry voice.

"What are you doing? Look what your kid has done!"

I looked up. The fat lady was standing up now with her hands on her hips. Her face was all crumpled, and on her bulbous, purple bottom lip you could see a disgusting bubble of spit. I looked at Charlie.

At first I thought he was sitting on a rug, except that this one appeared to be made of knickers. Red pants, blue pants, black pants, stripy pants. Charlie, meanwhile, had chosen a pair with spots on like a leopard, and was stretching them over his head. Although he didn't need to stretch them much because they were enormous, like a big spotty tent. You could just see his grinning face through a leg hole.

"Charlie!" scolded Mummy. "Put those back at once!"

The fat woman bent down and snatched her pants from Charlie's head, and started to stuff them all back through the broken zip.

"I'm so sorry," said my Mummy, "I think he was just being curious. Charlie, say sorry to the lady."

"Sorry lady," said naughty Charlie, not sounding at all sorry.

"People like you need to keep your children under control," said the woman.

"Now hang on a second," said Mummy, "he was only -".

But Daddy put his hand on her arm, and in a flash he stepped in front of Mummy and scooped Charlie up into his arms.

"He's very sorry, and we are too. Aren't we, Cheeky Charlie?" and he smiled his big Daddy smile, and ruffled Charlie's hair.

*   *   *

Later on, as we walked across the tarmac towards the plane, we found ourselves behind the funny couple again. As they headed for the front staircase, Mummy pulled Daddy's arm and steered us all towards the back.

On board, the seats were nearly full. "It cost us fifteen quid to get on first," grumbled Daddy as we waited for people to sit down. "Fat lot of good that turned out to be."

"Well I explained as fast as I could," replied Mummy in the voice she uses when she's going to get really angry, really quickly. "If someone had been watching Charlie properly this morning, he wouldn't have put all those knives and forks into my handbag, would he? And then Mummy wouldn't have had to answer all those questions when the security alarm went off." She pulled me to one side.

"Come on Harry, let's sit here."

We sat down in two seats, with Daddy and Charlie sitting several rows further forward. I got myself comfy and Mummy gave me a sweet from her handbag.

"Shall I give one to the boys?" she asked me. I shook my head.

"No, I agree. These sweets are only for girls," and she gave me a little cuddle.

I'm going to skip the next bit because the flight was very long, and very boring. I could hardly see the telly from my seat, and in any case it was showing a grown-up TV programme. You could hear the sound of people laughing, but I don't know why because the people weren't doing anything funny.

Later, after they'd given us our lunch, Mummy nudged me. "Look at that," she said smiling. One of the pretty waitresses was talking to Charlie. Daddy was looking at the waitress, grinning.

Just then she got up to let someone past – it was the fat lady. Inside the aeroplane, she looked fatter than ever: her legs bish-bashed people's elbows and bumped their shoulders. She was grabbing the top of each seat as if she was climbing a ladder.

She pushed her way past the waitress who nearly fell into Daddy's lap, but she didn't say sorry. "What a vile woman," I heard Mummy mutter just after she'd gone past.

Just then Charlie started pulling on Daddy's sleeve, and they both got up. Daddy looked towards us and mouthed the word "toilets". Mummy pulled a funny face and pointed towards the front of the plane, and off they went.

Mummy and I didn't see what happened next, but Daddy told us later. There was a queue for the toilet, so Daddy and Charlie waited in the aisle. While Daddy chatted to another waitress, Charlie had gone exploring – and found the skinny man fast asleep with his mouth open, like he was at the dentist. The seat next to him was empty, but on the tray in front of it was the fat woman's dinner, all ready to eat.

I bet you can guess what happened. You're right: Charlie plonked himself down and started eating. First he ate the chocolate pudding – but he was still hungry. Then he ate the biscuits – but he was still hungry. He even ate the carrots. Then he pushed all the mashed potato onto the tray with his fingers, and tried to make a 'well' for the gravy, just like Mummy does for the egg when she's making a cake. But he must have left a gap, because the gravy came running out when he poured it on top. Only the tray stopped it pouring all over the seat.

I'll tell you one thing Charlie didn't eat: the lump of cheese. He doesn't like cheese, but he thought the skinny man would. Or perhaps he thought it would give him funny dreams, like Mummy says. Whatever he was thinking, Charlie plonked this big lump of smelly yellow cheese straight into the skinny man's mouth.

Has anyone ever dropped cheese into your mouth when you are asleep? Me neither, but I bet it's not nice. The skinny man didn't like it because he woke up straight away, coughing and spluttering.

Other passengers around started to say "There, there,"

and offered him water. But then he started saying some very rude words so they said "OK mate calm down," and "I've got children here, do you mind?" and they went back to their dinners.

That's when Daddy noticed Charlie. Smeared with chocolate and mashed potato, he was climbing back into the aisle and running towards him.

Daddy did that scoopy-uppy thing again with Charlie, and just in time because the fat woman had just returned to her seat. Can you guess how happy she was to find that her dinner was gone?

Daddy told Mummy later that the fat woman was 'apoplectic'.

"Can I have a popple lectic?" asked Charlie.

"What does it mean, Daddy?" I asked.

"It means you are very, very angry," said Daddy.

"Very very very very very very angry," repeated Charlie. "Very very very very - "

"That's enough, Charlie," said Daddy, ruffling his hair. "You've got us into quite enough trouble already today, Your Cheekiness."

Charlie wasn't listening. How do I know? Because he did one more very naughty thing I'll tell you about before I go and have my tea.

*   *   *

It happened when we were waiting for our bags. Dad said he was desperate for a wee, so Mummy, Charlie and I waited by the conveyor belt. Have you ever seen one? They're really cool; they go round and round with the luggage, and if you're lucky some of the bags fall off at the corners.

This conveyor belt came out through a hole in the wall, went around a big loop, and then disappeared again. The holes were covered in long flaps, a bit like the doors at the back of supermarkets where you're not supposed to go.

I'll tell you about Charlie getting lost in the supermarket another time, but the important bit of that story is that they found him on the other side of the flaps, trying to open a jumbo packet of Wotsits.

Who knows, maybe he thought he'd find some more Wotsits in the airport? I looked up to see him lying on his tummy on a big blue suitcase, with his arms and legs stretched out like Superman. He disappeared through the flaps head first with his feet kicking a little bit, as if he wanted to go faster.

"Mummy! Look at Charlie!" And I pointed.

"What?" said Mummy, who was reading her book.

"He went through the hole on a bag!" I explained. Mummy told me not to move an inch, and she started running towards the end of the belt.

Before she could get there, the flaps started to lift up where the bags come out. It was a big black case... and on it sat Charlie! He was cross-legged, just like you have to do in assembly. He looked very pleased with himself, and you must admit it was a clever trick to swap cases so quickly.

But right at that moment, a big pair of hairy arms came through the flaps, and pulled him back! I screamed. I heard Mummy scream too, and she started climbing onto the conveyor belt.

"Mummy watch out, he'll get you too!" I yelled.

But Mummy didn't go through the flaps. Instead she climbed right over the belt, and was now in the middle of the loop, clambering over all the adverts.

She had one leg on each side of a woman holding a plate of salad when a door next to the belt opened. Through it came a giant man in blue overalls, carrying Charlie in his arms. Both of them were smiling. The man pressed the big red button on the wall and the conveyor belt made a groaning noise and stopped.

Mummy must have been quite tired from her climbing because she was really red and sweaty by the time she got back to me, just at the same time as Daddy got back from the toilet.

"What's the matter with you?" asked Daddy.

"Don't even go there," said Mummy, although she wasn't pointing at the hole in the wall, so I did, to help Daddy. "Just don't even go there."

"Charlie been playing up again, has he?" said Daddy. Hair ruffle. "What a Cheeky Charlie you are."

Water slides

Have you ever stayed in a hotel? We have. It was last year, in the summer. We flew to Spain in an aeroplane. It was night when we arrived. As we stood at the top of the steps waiting to get off you could feel the warm wind on your face, and there was a funny smell, too. "Just like one of Daddy's trumps, but nicer," said Mummy.

But forget about that, because I want to tell you about the amazing hotel. There was a machine where you could buy crisps and drinks whenever you wanted, and a restaurant where you could have cherry yoghurt and ham for breakfast, every morning. And if you wanted toast, you had to do it yourself: you put the bread onto this special thingy and it slid into the toaster automatically, moving along like your shopping does at the checkout in Asda. And then you rushed around to the other end and it slid out of the machine, all nice and toasty!

We only used it for a few days, though, because halfway through our holiday there was a big sign on the toaster saying 'No funciona', which means 'Not working" in Spanish. It was turned on its side with lots of springs and metal bits hanging out. Next to it, on the tray, were all sorts of blackened, twisted things that had been put through the toaster.

Charlie and I poked around: we could see a plastic spoon, a piece of someone's sunglasses, one of those special cards that you use to get into hotel bedrooms instead of keys, and...

"Is my hellyfant!" said Charlie, picking up a lump of stinky grey plastic.

Now most children would be very grumpy if their favourite toy was ruined – even if it was their fault, because they had been trying to make elephant on toast. Not Charlie.

"Look my hellyfant is all melty!" he shouted, and he ran back to Mummy with a big smile on his face.

I saw her look at the lump. She looked at the toasting machine. And then she shook her head. With a big smile on his face, Charlie put his melty hellyfant into the change bag.

But the best thing about our hotel wasn't the toaster, it was the swimming pool. I don't know what the swimming pool in your town is like, but the one near my house is boring. It's a rectangle with ropes in it, and grown-ups swim from end to end looking like they need a poo. You can't run, you can't jump, you can't splash. Bor-ring.

But not the one at this hotel. For a start it was shaped like a jelly that has been dropped on the floor, with curvy edges and extra little blobby pools around the outside that Mummy said were called Jacuzzis, but Charlie called 'bubble baths'. And then all around, raised up on stilts and starting high up at the top of a tower, were two twisty, turny waterslides: a blue one called The Hamster, and a green one called The Dragon.

The Hamster was long and slow. It was like a tube cut in half, and people waved at their friends as they travelled on the special mats around the spaghetti bends and down the steep bits. At the end it plopped you out into one of the big pools next to the stairs, so you could run up and have another go.

But The Dragon was very different. Apart from the first bit, this one was a proper tube: you couldn't see out. Even at the start, the place where you put your mat, it was really steep and fierce jets of water squirted out right next to your bottom.

On the first day we sat in the chairs by the pool, and you could see people holding on to the bars at the top and trying to sit on their mats. But the water made them slip, and they usually disappeared into the tube sideways or backwards, screaming. Then you heard them scream some more as they went around the bends. At the bottom they shot out of a dragon's mouth into the main pool, right in front of everyone, still screaming. They made a massive 'kersploosh!' as they landed, and went right under the water. That usually stopped people screaming.

Even though I'm really good at swimming, I didn't want to go on The Dragon. I was a bit afraid of The Hamster too, which is strange because I'm not afraid of real hamsters, even when they do a wee on my school uniform like my friend's hamster does.

"It's just like the slides at the soft play, but with water," said my Daddy as we all sat in one of the Jacuzzis later on.

"It's *nothing* like the soft play," I said. "For a start, it's outside. For another start, there are lots of big boys on it," I continued, pointing at The Hamster.

Some boys had managed to stop half way down, and they were using their mats to hold up the water like a dam. Then one of the hotel people pointed at them and blew a whistle. So they lifted their mats and let all the water go with a whoosh!, and they then jumped onto the wave they had made, shouting and whooping all the way to the bottom.

Meantime, back in our Jacuzzi, Charlie was trying to press the button to turn on the bubbles. He only has chubby little fingers so I reached over and pressed it for him.

"No I wanna do it!" he screamed, right in my face.

I stuck my tongue out at him, and he screamed again. He's really easy to annoy, sometimes.

Mummy was just telling him to calm down when the bubbles started. They came out of everywhere: by your feet, on your back, even up your bum a bit when you sat in the special seats. The water turned completely white with bubbles, so you couldn't even see your knees.

"Check me out!" said Daddy, who was floating on his back. Unlike all the boys on the slide who were wearing tight swimming trunks, Daddy was wearing massive blue shorts with pink flowers on them – his 'baggies', he called them.

Something odd was happening. Daddy's baggies were getting bigger. Much, much bigger. They were blowing up like James' Giant Peach, or a hot air balloon.

"Did you have beans for breakfast?" asked Mummy.

"Beans, beans, good for your heart, the more you eat the more you fart!" I shouted. My friend Jade taught me that. Only you couldn't hear the last bit because Mummy put her hand over my mouth.

By now Daddy's shorts were so big, it looked like he was going to explode. He poked them, and they puffed straight back up again.

Do you ever do pile-ons with grown-ups? It's where you all shout "Pile on!" and climb on top of them, and if you're at the bottom you can hardly breathe and you have to scream until they get off.

Charlie loves a pile-on, and from where he stood on the side, this looked like the perfect chance. Shouting "Pie Ron!" he threw himself right onto Daddy's inflatable shorts.

"Ooof!" shouted Daddy, as the weight of Charlie bent him in half.

"Cool!" I shouted.

"Oh Charlie," sighed Mummy.

Charlie probably shouted something else too, but we didn't hear him because he had disappeared under the bubbles.

Quick as a flash, Daddy reached under the water, scooped him out and sat him on his lap. Water was running down his face, which Charlie hates.

"That was a bit daft, wasn't it Charlie?" said Daddy, giving him a cuddle.

Charlie sniffed a bit, then went quiet.

"I done a wee," he said quietly.

"I think it's time for us to get out now," said Mummy firmly.

*   *   *

After we'd had a toasted sandwich in the café, we went back out to the main pool. There were sun loungers lined up in a row, and we threw our towels over the ones at the end and climbed on.

"What are we going to do?" I asked.

"Well I don't know about you, but I'm going to catch some rays and have a kip," said Daddy, leaning back and closing his eyes.

"You can go and play," said Mummy, "but make sure you stay where I can see you." And she picked up her magazine.

We were by the pool where The Dragon ended, but nobody was coming down the slide. Grown-ups were just sitting around; some of them were reading, but many of them were asleep. It was hot, and there was nothing to do. I picked up Daddy's mirror sunglasses, and tried them on. They made everything look dark, like night was coming and it was nearly time for bed. Why would you want that?

"Do I look cool?" I asked Mummy, who just smiled and carried on reading. Charlie copied me. He's always copying me. Do you have a little brother or sister that does that? It drives me mad. He pulled Mummy's sunglasses off her face, and put them on. They were way too big, and kept falling off his nose.

"If you break those, I'm going to be hopping mad," said Mummy. That was a mistake, of course, because then Charlie started trying to hop round, and he screwed up his nose to make himself look mad. And the sunglasses fell onto the floor.

"Shoo!" said Mummy, picking them up and examining them for scratches. "Go and make mischief somewhere else, I'm off duty."

"That's a bit rude," I said. "Come on Charlie, let's explore."

I grabbed his hand and we walked along the edge of the pool.

Now here's something else that's really annoying about Charlie: everyone likes him. People smile at him, come up and pat his wavy, hairy head, or tell Mummy what a 'cutie' they think he is. And the thing is, Charlie doesn't even say thank you! He just stands there looking really serious, like he does when he's trying to decide which flavour milkshake he wants.

And this time was no different.

"Hello!" said the old lady on the blue towel.

"Hola!" said the woman on the red towel. (Hola means 'Hello' in Spain, my Mummy told me that.)

The man with the headphones winked at him instead, and made a 'chick-chick' sound out of the side of his mouth.

But Charlie just kept on walking, ignoring them all.

We got to the end of the row of sun loungers, and the last one was empty. I sat down, but Charlie crawled underneath and started to tickle my legs.

"Charlie! Stop it!" I said. You're not at home now, get out!"

At home, Charlie is always crawling under the table. He'll sit there pretending to be a dog and licking your knee, or chewing the laces on your shoes. Once, when Mummy had lots of friends for tea, he started to shout out what colour pants Mummy's friends were wearing. "Blue pants! Black pants! Black pants again!" he'd said, and all Mummy's friends had started screaming with laughter.

"Little pants! Big pants!" he'd continued, but then he started getting silly, like he always does. "Stinky pants! Poo poo pants! She got no pants on!"

At that point Mummy had pulled him out from under the table, and asked him to say sorry to her friends with the stinky pants and the poo poo pants. The woman with no pants on said that he had made a mistake, and that they were just too small for Charlie to see.

So it wasn't a surprise when Charlie climbed under my sun lounger. I found something to do, anyway, because I realised you can dip your toe into the pool and then draw pictures on the tiles in water. They fade quite quickly, but you just get your toe wet and do it again.

I'm not sure how long I was painting pictures for, but I stopped when a man got out of the pool and walked his wet, hairy monster feet right over my painting, ruining it. I looked up to see Charlie, and realised that he'd crawled all the way back to Mummy and Daddy, through the tunnel of sun loungers.

As I walked back towards them, the first woman I walked past was looking for something, and muttering angrily to herself. As she did so, the next woman put on a pair of sunglasses, and the first woman started pointing at her face, and getting shouty.

I moved on. On the next sun lounger was a sleeping man, and he was wearing a hat. This was no ordinary hat. It was large, with a floppy rim, and it was bright pink. I've never seen a man wearing a bright pink hat before.

Just along from him was another woman, reading a book. I nearly tripped over her shoes, and that was hardly surprising because they were huge. They were blue Crocs, and they looked like canoes. My Grandad has massive feet, but these were extraordinary.

But it didn't make sense: this woman, asleep on her sun lounger, was tiny! Her little legs ended in little feet with little painted toes. It seemed a shame she couldn't get shoes the right size.

Next to her were an English man and woman who had sat near us at breakfast. The woman was doing that thing where women lie on their front and undo their tops. I don't know why they do that, perhaps the straps are a bit itchy. The man was putting suncream on her back. But just as he picked up the bottle to squeeze some out, the woman with the tiny feet reached out and snatched it out of his hand!

"Oi! What do you think you're playing at?" he shouted.

Tiny toes shouted something back in Spanish that I didn't understand, but I don't think she was asking if he liked cherry yoghurt for breakfast.

"What's the matter, Gary?" asked the woman, twisting her neck round to see.

"This nutter has just stolen our suncream!" said Gary, pointing at tiny toes. "Seriously, she just grabbed it!"

"But Gary, that's not our suncream," said the woman. "Ours is from Boots."

"It must be," said Gary. "It was under my towel!"

Tiny toes was now standing besides the British woman. She had her hands on her hips and a very red face. Perhaps she did need more suncream after all.

"You wan my suncream?" she said. "Here, have my suncream," and she took the top off the bottle and poured the white liquid out all over the woman's back. It went everywhere, splashing off onto her red towel and dripping onto the ground.

Have you ever dropped a vanilla ice cream? I have. Mummy had to cut bits off it that might have touched dog poo, and then she scooped the rest back into my cone with her fingers. It still tasted the same. Anyway, that's what this suncream looked like, splooshed all over the place.

"Aaargh! What the..." said the woman, and she lifted herself up. But then she remembered that she hadn't got her top on, so she snatched her red towel to wrap it round her, tipping loads of her stuff onto the ground.

"Watch out Soph, that's my phone!" said the man as his shiny mobile clattered onto the tiles.

"That's not your phone, Gary. Not unless you've bought a Minnie Mouse case. Why have you got someone else's phone?"

Something seriously strange was going on, and it was happening to everyone I walked past, although I must admit I did slow down a bit to hear what people were saying. 'Stop gawping,' my Mummy says when I do this, but she's as nosy as anybody so I take no notice.

Anyway, people all around the pool were talking now, and pointing at each other. I hurried past a man who was wearing big pink sunglasses, and another man who was telling his friend, "No but seriously, I put the car keys just there. If we can't find them, we're stuffed. We should call the police."

Finally, I was back with Mummy and Daddy. I watched as people argued, swapped sunglasses, lifted up their sun loungers and emptied their bags.

"Why has everyone got ants in their pants?" asked Daddy.

"I'm not sure," said Mummy, "but... Charlie, does this have anything to do with you?"

Charlie was looking at the sky, picking his nose.

"Charlie? I'm talking to you. Have you been up to your shenanigans again?"

Slowly, Charlie put his finger in his mouth, sucked it, and smiled a big smile. "I want nanny kittens!" he said. "I love nanny kittens!"

"Nanny kittens?" said Daddy. "What have kittens got to do with the price of fish?"

"Don't like fishies," said Charlie.

"Are we having fish tonight, Daddy?" I asked.

Mummy groaned, loudly. "Why can't you lot talk normally? Give me strength," she said. So Charlie ran over and started to squeeze her arm muscles.

Daddy sat up, and looked at the small crowd of people who were gathered halfway down the pool. They were talking, waving their hands, and some of them were pointing at us.

"I think it's about time we did a runner," said Daddy, quickly gathering up our things. "Come on kids, let's skedaddle."

"Ski?" I said. "And what's a daddle, Daddy?"

I was more confused than ever. Was Daddy talking Spanish?

"Never mind that now," said Daddy, pulling Charlie by the hand. "I'll explain later. Let's get out of here."

As Charlie got to his feet, there was a clinking sound, and a big bunch of car keys fell out of his shorts.

"Ow!" he said, as they landed on his toes.

Before we could say anything, Daddy gave them a little kick with the side of his foot and sent them skidding under our neighbour's sun lounger.

"Come on kids, time to explore," he announced, pulling us firmly by the hand away. "Nothing here for us to worry about."

*   *   *

"I'll tell you what," said Daddy as we walked past the tower, "let's go on the slides."

"Yay!" shouted Charlie. "I want go on The Dragon!"

"I am *not* going on The Dragon," I said.

"Me neither," said Mummy. "It looks horrific. And the kids are too small, Tom," said my Mummy.

"I'm not small I'm FREE!" shouted Charlie, stamping his foot.

"You may be three, but you're still not big enough. Maybe next year."

"Ah relax," said Daddy. "I'll go down with them. You can wait for us at the bottom."

"Yay! Yay-yay-yay! Yay-de-yay-yay!" shouted Charlie.

Have you noticed how much Charlie shouts? I once told Charlie that his belly button was actually a volume control, and I stuck my finger in it and twiddles it around to see if he'd be quiet. But then he shouted "Ow", so I told him his button must be broken.

So Mummy put a swimming jacket on Charlie and helped me put on my armbands, and then she took all our bags. We grabbed Daddy's hand and set off up the steps.

"One two three four five seven ten eleventy twenty," counted Charlie as we went up. He's rubbish at numbers.

"I reckon you could do The Dragon," said Daddy to me.

"But it looks really scary," I said. "I might get stuck in the tube."

"It's not like *Charlie and the Chocolate Factory* you know, Harry. And you're a skinny minnie, anyway. Come on, it'll be fun, and I'll hold you the whole way down."

"Only if you promise to lift me up at the end so I don't get water up my schnozz," I said. "Pinky promise."

"Pinky promise," said Daddy.

And so we climbed past the entrance to The Hamster, all the way to the top where The Dragon started.

We were seriously high. You could see right out of the hotel, over the roofs of the town towards the sea. The metal platform we were standing on had little gaps in it, and through them you could see people climbing up the steps underneath you. In front of us, two more steps led up to The Dragon; there were handles to grab onto so you could sit down and get yourself ready. You could just see the first bend, and the entrance to the green tunnel.

I grabbed the railing and looked down to see if I could see Mummy. Big mistake. My tummy felt funny straight away, the same feeling I get when Daddy drives over a humpy bridge. Does yours do that? It feels like your insides are rolling over and over, like socks in a washing machine.

I grabbed Daddy's arm tightly. "I'm scared," I said. Even Charlie was a bit quieter than normal. All you could hear were the jets of water, and the far-away cries of children in the swimming pools at the bottom.

"Ah come on," said Daddy. "It'll be brilliant."

"Now, how are we going to do this?" he said. "Perhaps I should have thought this through a little bit more," and he picked up a mat from the pile.

"I'll tell you what. I'll get onto the mat, and hold onto the bars. Then Charlie, you climb on first, and sit between my legs so you're at the front. Harry, you're on last. Climb over me into the middle, and grab Charlie round the waist. Easy peasy."

And before we could say anything he'd let go of our hands, climbed up the steps, and plonked himself down on his mat in the water jets at the top of the slide.

"Whoah, these babies are strong!" he said, grabbing onto the bars.

"What babies?" said Charlie.

"He means the jets," I said. Daddy's always talking about babies instead of the proper words. I don't know why.

"Right, Charlie boy, climb on board the Daddy train!"

Charlie clambered up the steps behind Daddy, and stood there, not quite knowing what to do.

"Just crawl over me," said Daddy, who grabbed the bar above his head with one hand, and took Charlie's arm with the other. Lying back flat, he let Charlie wriggle down his body towards the space on the mat at the front, between Daddy's knees. Everything was wet and slippery, and Charlie's little hands were grabbing and prodding, trying to get a grip.

"Ooh!" said Daddy as Charlie climbed on top.

"Fnurgh!" said Daddy as Charlie's knee squashed Daddy's nose.

"Aieee! Don't grab that!" said Daddy when Charlie grabbed hold of the hairs on Daddy's chest.

"Finally!" said Daddy as Charlie twizzled around, and sat himself down, grabbing Daddy's shorts to stop him sliding off down the tube.

"Right Harry, you're up. Do the same as Charlie, but try not to break every bone in my body," said Daddy.

I was seriously scared, but I didn't want to show it because there was now a big queue behind us, waiting for us to get going. So I took a big step over Daddy's head, and then swung my other leg over and sat down on Daddy's chest.

"Shuffle down!" said a voice from under my bottom.

So I did a bum shuffle forward, jumping down Daddy's tummy, making him groan some more.

I was nearly there, and I pushed myself forward one more time. Except that I pushed a bit too hard, because I thumped into the back of Charlie, grabbing him round his waist because I was too far from the handles to hold on any more.

"Harry!" he shouted. "Stop bumping me! I slipping!"

He was right, he was slipping. And he wasn't the only one either. Daddy's knees were trying to squash us to stop us sliding away, but the mat underneath us was moving too.

"Hold on Charlie!" shouted Daddy. "We're not ready!"

"I am holding on," shouted back Charlie.

Have I explained this properly to you? Daddy's holding onto the bars, trying to get comfy on the mat. I'm sat between his legs, holding onto Charlie. And Charlie is now sat on my lap, holding onto the ends of Daddy's shorts. And all the time, massive jets of water are trying to push us down the slide.

Now when Charlie grabs hold of something, you can't make him let go. It doesn't matter if it's your hand, a packet of mini Cheddars or – in this case – Daddy's shorts. But Daddy's shorts weren't so grabby. In fact, they gave up completely.

"Whoooooaaah!" said Charlie, and it was the right noise because we were off down the slide! Charlie, me, the mat and... Daddy's shorts. Without Daddy in them.

As we set off I turned to see him. He was still grabbing onto the metal bar, stretched out on his back with no clothes on, jets of water spraying all over him. He let go with one hand and tried to cover up his willy, but it was too late: the people in the queue were already howling with laughter, and pointing at him.

And that's all I saw, because Charlie and I were off! We zoomed into the tunnel and round the first bend, sliding half way up the walls on our mat, me and Charlie screaming like mad. And after that it just got faster, and more terrifying. We went round in a complete circle at one point, and I'm not sure but I think we might even have done a loop-the-loop.

But you know what was funny? At the top we were screaming because we were frightened. But by the bottom, when we plopped into the pool, we were screaming because we were having a great time. Same noise, different feeling.

Of course we did what everyone did when they come out of The Dragon, and went right under the water. But because I had my armbands on I bobbed straight back up, with Charlie next to me. We coughed and spluttered, and Charlie complained about the water in his eyes, but we splashed our way to the shallow end where Mummy was waiting with the towels.

A quick rub down and Charlie was off again.

"Don't go too far, Charlie!" said Mummy as he waddled away.

It was only then that we noticed the crowds of people

by the side of the pool, all pointing up at the top of the slide. I recognised lots of them – they were the same people who had been so angry when Charlie had mixed up their stuff.

But they weren't angry now. They were laughing, shouting, and taking pictures with their phones... of Daddy.

Because Daddy was still up there, hanging on. He'd somehow managed to grab another mat, and he was trying to wrap it around him like a towel. Except the water kept pushing it sideways and unrolling it, and he only had one hand to hold it.

As we watched, he lost his grip on the mat, and it zipped off down the slide. He let go of the bar, covered himself up with his hands, and followed the mat into the tunnel.

You could see his shadow as he went round the bends; we all followed him round and round, down and down, until he shot out at the bottom, feet first, still absolutely naked, into the pool.

Everyone, and I mean everyone, cheered.

"Smile for the camera!" shouted a man.

"I got you on YouTube!" shouted a boy waving a phone.

"Nice bum!" shouted a woman nearby. Mummy turned and gave her a funny look.

Daddy swam to the side, and waved to Mummy to bring a towel. She shook her head and smiled, and pointed to the steps. Daddy looked very grumpy, and waved again, so Mummy took a towel down. With one big push and a final flash of his white bottom, Daddy was up on the side and wrapped up.

Back by the sun loungers everyone calmed down and Daddy started to smile again.

"I'm glad I gave everyone a treat, anyway. Where are my shorts?" he said.

"Harry had them," said Mummy.

"No I didn't," I said, "Charlie did."

"Charlie?"

Charlie, who was back, stood and pointed. There, at the end of the tube and pulled right over the head of The Dragon, were Daddy's baggy, soggy shorts.

"I might have known. Cheeky Charlie," sighed Daddy, and he plodded off to get them, wrapped carefully in his towel.

Christmas Fair

"It's still wonky," I said. "And you've forgotten the big star on the top."

Daddy was putting up the Christmas tree, and he wasn't doing a very good job. Charlie wasn't helping either: he kept taking the shiny baubles from the box, putting them down his trousers and dancing around to the Christmas music until they rolled out by his shoes.

"Where's that star gone, then?" asked Daddy. "We had it last year."

I looked at Charlie. Charlie looked at me, with the funny face he uses when he's spilt his drink, broken something, or done a poo.

"That reminds me," Dad said to me, with a serious look on his face. "Did you know your grandad was a thief?"

"A thief?" I said. "Really? Which grandad? Did he go to prison?"

Mummy, who was making some gingerbread biscuits for the tree, looked up.

"Don't fall for it, Harry."

"I'm talking about your mum's dad," whispered Daddy, "Grandad Lou. He stole the stars from the sky, and he put them in your Mummy's eyes."

Mummy groaned, loudly.

"How can you steal the stars? What does that even mean?" I said to Daddy.

He sighed.

"Never mind. My shining wit is wasted on this family. Now bring me that grubby fairy with the missing leg, maybe we'll shove her on top instead... ah, Charlie! You've got the star. I might have known."

My little brother pulled the star out from under his jumper, and at last the tree was done.

I fetched my letter to Santa, which I had nearly finished, and put it under the tree for later. It's tricky, isn't it, deciding what you want. Here's what my letter said:

Dear Farther Crismas

I have been a gud girl this yer. Please can you gif me a scooter, sum new pens, a bag and

[Then I'd left a big space. Really big, about as big as my pencil case, so I could fill in some extra stuff later, when I thought of it.]

Lots of love Harriet xxxxxx

Charlie saw me, and ran into the lounge to fetch his letter too, shouting "Farmer Christmas! Farmer Christmas!" He's so silly.

Because he can't write, Mummy had given him a magazine and some glue. He'd ripped out pictures of the things he wanted for Christmas, and stuck them to a piece of paper. Here's what he chose:

- A bottle of perfume
- A ship
- A snowy mountain
- A lady's bottom wearing some funny pants
- And a mobile phone, just like Daddy's.

Can you imagine Santa trying to get down the chimney with a lady's bottom in his sack? I don't think so!

"Right," said Mummy. "These biscuits are done. Let's go to the fair."

"Yay!" Charlie and I cheered. We were off to the Christmas fair at my school.

Do you have fairs at your school? They're brilliant, aren't they? You get to go into loads of classrooms, even the Year 6 ones. I once went into the staffroom, too. You can decorate biscuits, win jars of sweets, and even run in the corridors.

It was busy at the fair. I mean really, really busy. The noise in the school hall was a bit scary at first. If we made that much noise in assembly, it would make Mr Bartlett, our head teacher, so mad his head would probably go pop. There were grown-ups everywhere, sitting on children's chairs and talking, and children running around between them.

It was nearly lunchtime, so we zig-zagged our way to the hatch where I normally get my baked potato-if-I-have-a-blue-band, or pasta-if-I-have-a-yellow-band. But I never wear a green band because I don't like vegetables except broccoli and sometimes peas.

This time though, they were selling massive sausage rolls. Why don't we get those for school dinner? It's not fair. Anyway, Mummy bought one for everyone, and we made our way to an empty table that Daddy had found, saying 'excuse me excuse me excuse me' all the way.

The sausage rolls were *scrumdiddlyumptious* (I learned that word in carpet time last week). As I was munching mine, I noticed that Charlie, who was standing at the end of the table, was nibbling all the pastry off the outside – just like I do with the chocolate on KitKats. He saw me watching him.

"Is for later," he said quietly.

Sure enough, when he had finished he took the huge,

wobbly pink bar of sausage meat, still with little bits of white pastry stuck to it, and put it down the back of his trousers!

"I got no pockets," he explained.

But just as he was finishing his sentence, Daddy came up behind him.

"Let's get you sat down properly, little one," he said, before lifting him by the armpits.

"No Daddeeeeeee!" I shouted, but it was too late. Flumph! He plopped Charlie down onto one of the chairs.

Straight away, tears started rolling down Charlie's cheeks.

"What on earth is the matter?" said Mummy crossly.

Charlie reached down his trousers, and pulled out a handful of squished pink sausage meat.

Mummy let out a little yelp, the kind of noise that my cousin's dog makes if you tread on his paw by accident, and everyone on the other tables turned to see what was going on.

*   *   *

A bit later, after I'd explained and Mummy had taken Charlie to the toilet to scrape the lunch off his bottom, we went exploring.

"Can I go on my own?" I asked.

"Yes, but you'll need to take Charlie with you," said Mummy. "Make sure he doesn't leave the hall, or get into trouble."

Well, I don't know if you've ever tried to look after a 3-year-old, but it's boring. And impossible. They run off, they squeeze into tiny gaps, they stop you talking to your friend Delilah. That's what Charlie did. So I thought, well I'll just tell Delilah what I'm getting for Christmas, then I'll find Mummy and tell her that Charlie is lost.

I was just showing Delilah my new rainbow bracelet, when I heard someone shouting. Then another voice, then a woman screaming, and this time it was a proper scream.

I looked across to where all the noise was coming from, near the Christmas tree in the corner. At first I couldn't see what was happening: lots of people were pointing at the wall. But then I spotted... well, can you imagine who it was?

Yep, Charlie. But he wasn't where you'd expect. You see the walls of our hall have bars on them that the older children use for climbing during PE. And Charlie is a good climber – a very good climber. In fact he'd got right to the top, higher than I've ever seen, up near the ceiling.

And it gets worse: he was only holding on with one chubby hand. The other? That was reaching out towards the star on the top of the Christmas tree.

And what was everyone else doing? That's a good question. All these grown-ups, the people who are always telling me what to do, were standing there, looking and pointing. Several of them had their mouths open, and I could even see what they were eating. Yuck.

But it didn't last long because quick as a flash, Mrs Buckle, the Year 3 teacher I hope I get next year, raced up the bars to reach him. It was amazing, because Mrs Buckle is very plump (Mummy won't let me say she's fat, even though she is). I've never even seen her walk quickly, but here she was, climbing the bars like a chubby monkey wearing a flowery dress.

She was just in time, because Charlie couldn't hold on any longer. He kind-of-fell, kind-of-slid down on top of Mrs Buckle, who grabbed him with one arm and pressed him into her chest. And Mrs Buckle has a very big chest: his head almost disappeared between her boobies.

Then two of the dads were up alongside her, supporting them both as she climbed down to the bottom.

Suddenly everyone was cheering, shouting and clapping, and someone even did a big whistle. Mummy hugged Charlie, and I squeezed through to join them.

"Are you OK?" asked Mummy, but Charlie was crying too much to reply.

Now I'm pretty sure that if I climbed the bars, Mummy would be really, really cross. But as you should know by now, normal rules don't apply to Charlie. Instead Mummy picked him up and gave him lots of cuddles while she spoke to Mr Bartlett.

Eventually, I dragged her away. I had important things I wanted to do, and Charlie was stopping me.

*   *   *

The queue to see Santa was massive. But by this time Daddy had come back from somewhere, and Mummy had explained everything, and Daddy had given Charlie a hug he didn't deserve, and we were nearly at the front.

*   *   *

But WAIT A MINUTE. I need you to stop reading. Do you really want to read any further? Because to tell the rest of this story about Charlie, I need to explain all about Father Christmas. And I mean everything. So if you are in Year 1 or something like that, you need your Mummy or Daddy to say it's OK for you to finish the story.

Have you checked it's OK? Good. That means you're old enough to know the secret – maybe you already do. But I have to be careful, because my Mummy always stops me when I talk about this at home, saying I must not "spoil the surprise" for Charlie.

So here we go. Here's an easy question for you. Do you think that the blow-up Santa that some shops have in the window is real? Of course not, it's just a toy. Charlie thinks it is, but that's because he's only three.

Here's a harder question. If you wore a Father Christmas outfit, would that make you Father Christmas? No, of course not! That's just dressing up. You knew that, didn't you?

And now the last question, I promise. When you see Santa on the telly, or in the shopping centre or the supermarket, is it always the *real* Father Christmas? If you think it is, you should stop reading NOW!

But if you know it isn't *always* the real Father Christmas then you're really clever like me. You're probably in Year 2 or even higher. And you're definitely a girl. Or maybe a very clever boy.

Because clever children like us know that even if it's just a make-believe Father Christmas, you have to pretend it's the real one. That way you'll still get a good present – but of course it won't be on your list, because only the real Father Christmas has that.

So that's what I was doing, as we went into see him. The teachers had turned Miss White's office into a grotto with spray snow on the windows and fairy lights round the door. And guarding that door was Mrs Wood, the Year 5 teacher; she was dressed up like an elf, although I've never seen an elf drinking tea and eating biscuits before.

It was our turn. Mrs Wood took me and Charlie by the hand, and led us into the office. There was Father Christmas, waiting for us. He looked real. He even sounded real. But I spotted a few clues.

For a start, he was wearing glasses, but not just any glasses: these had 'Red or dead' written on the side, just like the ones that Ellie's dad wears: I'd noticed it because that's a funny thing to have on your glasses, although maybe not for Father Christmas. And perhaps Father Christmas goes to the same shop as Ellie's dad anyway.

Then there was his bag, which was tucked behind his

chair. Not his sack of presents: that was next to the door, behind Mrs Wood the tea-drinking elf. This was his private bag, and it was bright yellow with green writing, just like the one that Ellie's dad carries to the train station in the morning. Hmm.

Charlie was telling Santa that he wanted a ship and some perfume for Christmas. While they talked I noticed that Santa's bag was open, and full of his stuff. I could see a lunchbox with some sandwiches in it, a mobile phone, and something else, too: a car magazine.

Now here's another question for you. (Sorry, I know I said there weren't any more questions, but I forgot about this one). Would Santa be interested in cars? No! You can't drive a normal car on snow. If it was a magazine about reindeers, or presents, then maybe. But it wasn't. So there was no way this was the real Santa.

But I pretended not to see, and then Charlie and I swapped chairs. Santa asked me if I'd been a good girl. I said yes, of course. He asked me if I was looking forward to Christmas. I said yes, of course. And he asked me what I wanted to get, and I told him a scooter.

And then it was over. Charlie, who was crawling around on the floor, jumped up and ran to Mrs Wood, who gave us both a present. Mine was way too small to be a scooter.

*   *   *

"How was that? Fun?" asked Mummy when we came out.

"Charlie, you're not supposed to unwrap your present!" I said, because that's just what Charlie was doing.

"Oh Charlie," said Mummy. "Go on then Harry, open yours if you want."

I did want. Charlie had got a packet of coloured pencils, and he looked quite grumpy about it. I felt happy, because I didn't get them: coloured pencils are rubbish, they never work properly. I don't even know why they exist.

I got a Dora pencil case, which was quite nice actually.

Next stop: the secret present room. This one is brilliant: it's just for children, no grown-ups allowed. Mummy gave us 50p each, and Charlie and I went in.

Inside, it was even busier than the hall. There were lots of children, all wrapping up presents, and a few grown-ups to help you if you got stuck. We squeezed into spaces at the wrapping desks and I handed over my 50p. I got a bottle of pink bubble bath which will be perfect for Mummy.

It took me ages to wrap it, but Charlie took even longer: I heard him telling the grown-ups to 'go away'. How rude. And when we came out, Charlie had two presents… and still had his 50p! The presents were really badly wrapped, with lots and lots of Sellotape going all the way around.

"Who are they for?" asked Mummy.

"Is for Harry, and is for me," said Charlie.

"Oh thank you Charlie!" I said. "Can I open it now?"

"Not now," said Mummy. "Let's just put those away for later," and she put them away in the buggy. Boo.

*   *   *

Next stop was the 'Win a bottle' room. Daddy had turned up again, but by now the fair was nearly over, and there wasn't much left. Mummy let me pick three tickets, and Daddy let Charlie pick three, as well. If the number on your ticket ended in a 5 or a 0, then you won the prize with the same number on the table.

We opened mine first: only one of the three was a winner, and Daddy got a bottle of apple juice. He made a face at me, because he wanted the wine.

Now Charlie's turn. He handed Daddy his first ticket: it was a winner. The helper looked at the table but there was nothing on the matching spot, so she gave him a bottle of beer from behind the desk. Big smile from Daddy.

Ticket number two was another winner. But again, there was nothing on the matching spot. The helper frowned, but again she gave Daddy a bottle from behind the desk: more beer. An even bigger smile from Daddy.

Ticket number three was another winner!

"You really are my lucky little elf, Charlie," said Daddy, patting him on the head as he waited for the helper, who was talking to the other grown-up: Mr Jones, the deputy head teacher.

"Can I just see what's in your hand?" said Mr Jones, bending down to Charlie.

Charlie grinned, and opened his podgy fist. In it there were hundreds of tickets, all scrumpled up.

"Charlie, where did you get all those?" asked Daddy.

Charlie pointed at the bin behind the bottle table. The same bin where the helper had been putting all the winning tickets.

"And where are the three tickets you chose?" continued Daddy, sounding a bit sad now.

Charlie lifted his foot: underneath, there were three tickets.

"Ah," said Daddy, putting his bottles of beer back on the table. "Slight problem. Sorry about that. You'll want these back, I think, and I also think it's time we went home."

And he pushed us all out of the room: I think he was worried that Mr Jones would call the police because Charlie had cheated.

*   *   *

The fair was over: everyone was going home. We shuffled out slowly, and walked around past the staffroom towards our car. Guess who I saw through the window? Father Christmas! He was talking to Mr Bartlett, and he looked really cross. Like I said, I'm pretty certain it wasn't the real Santa. I don't think Santa gets cross.

Getting in the car took ages, as always. Charlie was moaning and crying, I couldn't do my seat belt up, and Daddy was starting to get grumpy.

"OK, all set?" he said, and started the engine. Just then, we heard 'Jingle Bells' playing. Now in our car, when the engine starts, the radio often comes on, and that's what I thought it was.

Charlie thought so too, and started singing: "Bingle Jells, Bingle Jells, Bingle awwl the way!"

But then the music stopped. And then started again.

"What is that music?" asked Daddy.

"I don't know, it sounds like something in the back," said Mummy.

"Take a look, will you," said Daddy, and Mummy sighed, got out and opened the boot.

"It's getting louder!" I shouted, as Mummy moved stuff around.

"It's something in the buggy," she said. "It's this present!" she cried, holding up the one that Charlie had wrapped for himself. "Charlie, what have you got here?" and she started unwrapping it.

"No no no no no!" cried Charlie.

"But seriously Charlie, this is a mobile phone!" said Mummy, pulling it out of the Sellotape. "Where on earth did you get this?"

Charlie said nothing, and looked at his feet.

"That's a new iPhone – someone will be missing that," said Daddy. "Just answer it, love, you'll find out soon enough."

"Umm, hello?" said Mummy. I didn't know who it was, but I could hear they were quite angry. "Oh hello Jim, it's Harry's mum here. Yes it is, I'm not quite sure how we've ended up with it, but I think it might have been something to do with Charlie... I'm so sorry," she said. "Of course, I'll drop it round on the way home. I really am very sorry."

She put the phone into her pocket.

"Who was it Mummy? Who's Jim?"

"Well," said Mummy. "I don't quite know how to say this, but Charlie knows who's phone it is, don't you Charlie?"

Charlie sniffed, and in a very small voice he whispered, "Is Farmer Christmas phone."

"No, seriously?" said Daddy. "You took Santa's mobile? From his grotto? I don't know if I should laugh or drop you off at the police station!"

And that, it seemed, was that.

"Ellie's dad will find a way to get it back to Santa," said Mummy, but by now I think we all know the truth about my school Father Christmas, don't we?

Charlie was still sniffing, and Daddy was still chuckling. "Nicked Santa's phone, just wait until I speak to Jim," said Daddy. "Charlie, it may be Christmas, but you are bad for my elf. Bad for my elf, do you get it? Elf, get it? Sounds like health? Elf?"

Everyone in the car was silent.

"Ah, never mind," said Daddy, and started the engine. "I don't know why I bother."

PS I almost forgot: can you guess what was in my present from Charlie? It was those coloured pencils, of course. They're rubbish, but then you knew that, didn't you?

Soft play

It was the really boring week just after Christmas, the worst one in the world when you can't go out because it's raining, and you don't want to stay in because everyone is so annoying. I watched the CBeebies Panto about 134 times, even though it's a bit babyish for me. Charlie was running around shouting nonsense, Mummy was shouting at Charlie, and Daddy said he was doing 'something important' on the computer.

"I'm bored," I said to Mummy.

"All aboard!" shouted Charlie, and made a whistling noise like a train.

Mummy turned to me. "You know what they say, Harry, only boring people get..."

"...bored, yes I know, you always say that!" I replied.

"Say dat! Say dat! Say dat!" chanted Charlie, marching up and down the hall, waving his arms and stomping his feet.

"Can we go to the park?" I asked, but I knew the answer already because I could hear the rain gurgling out of the drainpipe by the front door.

"Not a chance," said Mummy, "...but I suppose we could go to Our Space, if you want?"

"Yay!" I shouted.

"Arse face! Arse face! Arse face!" shouted Charlie.

"Charlie!" scolded Mummy. "Just because Daddy says something doesn't mean you should copy him."

I need to explain. Our Space – or Arse Face, as Daddy and I like to call it – is the soft play place near us. Have you got one of those near you? Does it have a bumpy slide, and a curly wurly one too that's all dark and scary? I go down them on my own now. It's brilliant.

So I put my shoes on, Mummy changed Charlie's nappy and shoved it into the stinky bag in the hall, and we got ready to go. It always takes ages, and this time was no different with people running in and out of the front door, putting stuff in the car and shouting at each other.

"Seriously love, what do you keep in this change bag?" said Daddy. "It weighs a ton."

"Just the essentials," said Mummy. "Now come on, let's go before it's too late."

We left, at last. I don't know why grown-ups make such a fuss.

When we got there it was really noisy: a girl was

having a Disney Princess birthday party in the side room, and girls kept running in and out. Most of them had long blonde flicky hair, and they were all wearing pink party t-shirts with a big number 8 on the front and BELLA on the back.

One of the mums came out and shouted out that the balloon man was here, and that all of Isabella's friends should go to see him do his tricks. The girls in the pink t-shirts ran inside.

"Are those people made of money?" muttered Mummy as we wiggled through the tables.

"I think it looks brilliant," I said. "I wish I was invited."

"Rubbish," replied Mummy. "Your party in the park was much better. You played hide and seek, remember?"

Mummy seriously thinks that hide and seek was better than a princess party at Arse Face. I don't think so!

We put the bags down at a spare table, and immediately Charlie ran off.

"Charlie! Don't go too..." Mummy starts to say. "Oh well," she continued, "I'm sure he'll be fine. Keep an eye out for him will you Harry? Who knows where he'll end up."

Well I had better things to do than chase around looking for Charlie. I wandered over and sat on the baby climbing frame, just outside the party room. I could hear all the girls inside, laughing and giggling. They were giggling a lot, in fact: the magic man must have been really funny. I wished I was at the party.

OK, this was weird, now they were shouting. And one of them was screaming.

The door opened, and one of the mums stood there. Her face was bright pink, just like the girls' t-shirts.

"It's time you went back to your parents, wherever they are," she said crossly, in a really posh voice. "And put those presents down."

Behind her, I could just make out the face of her uninvited guest – it was Charlie, of course. He was hard to see, because his top half was hidden behind an armful of things: rainbow bands, colouring books, some clothes, even a robot dog. Meanwhile his bottom half was mostly covered up by a mountain of wrapping paper, all torn and crumpled.

"Seriously, put those things down immediately, before I call for your mummy," said the posh woman.

For once, Charlie did as he was told. But because it was Charlie, he just opened his arms wide, and all the presents fell into the pile of wrapping paper with a giant clatter. He stepped carefully over the pile, and walked out of the room with a cheeky smile.

*   *   *

Charlie ran straight past me, and I wasn't going to get told off for hanging around, so I jumped down and went across to the climbing equipment for big children. I climbed right to the very top – you have to go through the ball pit, up the main tower, across the rope bridge and up the little tower next to the bumpy slide.

From there I could see everything: Mummy was sat at the table, playing with her phone; Daddy was buying coffee and hopefully a snack for me, too; and Charlie... well he was around somewhere. Probably causing trouble again.

Ah, there he was, coming towards the ramp where you get into the climbing area. Except he was walking in a really weird way, sideways like a crab, because he was dragging the change bag behind him. He really is quite a strange boy. Do you have a brother? I hope that if you do, he's a bit strange too, because then you'll know how I feel.

I whizzed down the bumpy slide, feeling glad that I'd put my slippy-slidey leggings on this morning. It was getting busier, so it took me ages to get back to Mummy, who gave me a finger of Kit Kat. I waved at Charlie to see if he wanted one but he was half-way up the tower, and wasn't looking.

"Where's the change bag?" asked Mummy.

Daddy didn't answer, and I carried on trying to bite all the chocolate off my Kit Kat finger without nibbling the wafer bit.

"No but seriously, where is it?" she said.

"I think I saw Charlie with it," I said. A big bit of chocolate dropped on the floor. I hate it when that happens.

"Why would Charlie have the change bag?" asked Mummy, "and where is he, anyway?"

"I saw him over there," I said, and pointed towards the entrance by the tower, where a crowd of children were standing around one of the Arse Face helpers.

Lots of the children were laughing and pointing up, but the woman looked 'a bit shirty', which is what my Mummy says when Daddy is a bit grumpy.

Then I saw what the children were pointing at. Or 'who' they were pointing at, because it was Charlie (of course). He was standing at the top of the tower, and wearing a 'nappy hat'. You do know what one of those is, don't you? It's when you get a clean nappy and put it on your head. You should try it, it's really funny. Just make sure it hasn't got poo in it otherwise you'll get it stuck in your hair.

But there was another reason why the children were pointing and laughing. As we watched, Charlie reached into the change bag by his feet and pulled out another nappy... except this one wasn't clean. It was all rolled up into a ball, like the smelly ones that Daddy throws down the stairs.

So then Charlie, who had a big grin on his face, did a little run and threw the nappy ball down the curly wurly slide. A few seconds later the children cheered as it came shooting out of the bottom and landed in the ball pool.

I'll tell you one person who wasn't cheering: the Arse Face woman. She was climbing up the tower, really quickly like a chimpanzee in the zoo. She was being chased by Mummy, who had run across and was catching up, three rungs at a time. Brilliant, they were having a race!

"Come on Mummy!" I shouted, but it was no good: the Arse Face woman got to the top first. It wasn't fair, she had a head start.

*   *   *

A bit later, when Charlie had come down with Mummy, and Daddy had finished getting a bit shirty with the Arse Face woman, Mummy decided it was time to leave anyway, and we all got into the car.

As we went round the roundabout, Charlie did what he always does, and shouted 'Old Macdonald's!' as soon as he saw the MacDonald's clown. Only this time you could hardly hear him speak, and he covered me in a spray of crumbs.

"Charlie, what are you eating?" said Mummy, turning around.

"Cake from my party bag," said Charlie, holding up a pink Disney Princess bag, and looking extremely pleased with himself.

"Oh Charlie," said Daddy, who was driving. "You really are a very naughty, very cheeky boy. Now give me a bit of that cake."

And he winked at Charlie in the mirror.

Hospital

When my Daddy was a little boy, his mummy died. Well, he wasn't *really* little, he says he was a teenager, so quite big actually. He says his mummy got a poorly tummy, and then she went to hospital, and then she died.

I think maybe I should feel sad about that, but I don't, because I never met her. If I look at the old photo of her on the landing I can make myself feel a bit sad, but not enough to cry. So I just make a sad face and say "Awww" and give Daddy a cuddle to make him feel better.

But Granny Fran, my mummy's mummy, is still really alive, even though she's very, very old. She's 143 or something like that, but she can still walk, and talk and do the shopping. But she's not very good at jumping sideways, which is what she should have done when the car went across the zebra crossing and bonked her on the leg.

She fell over, and an ambulance came and took her to hospital.

"Did it have its nee-naws on, Granny?" I asked her

afterwards.

"I don't know, dear. Yes, I think it did."

"Cool," I said, and Charlie ran up and down the room shouting "NEE NAW NEE NAW!" until Mummy told him to "put a sock in it", which was a silly thing to say because then Charlie started to eat his socks.

Anyway, we didn't find out about Granny's accident until Mummy took Charlie and me to see her in the hospital after school.

"Is she going to die?" asked Charlie.

"Don't be stupid, the car only hit her on the leg," I said, although I wasn't sure. After all, Daddy's mummy only had a tummy ache when she went to hospital.

"We don't say 'stupid' thank you, Harry," said Mummy, "and no, she's not going to die. She was very lucky, and she's just a bit shaken up, that's all."

Being hit by a car didn't sound lucky to me, but I stayed quiet, and soon we were walking up and down long hospital corridors, getting in and out of lifts, trying to find Granny.

Eventually we came to some big doors with a sign above them that I couldn't read. I asked Mummy what it said.

"Geriatrics," said Mummy. "That means medicine for old people."

"Jerry tricks?" shouted Charlie excitedly. "I love tricks. I want see Jerry. What tricks does Jerry do? Is he poorly? Can we see him now? Can he do balloon swords? Can he turn into a giraffe? Will I..."

"Enough, Charlie," said Mummy. "Let's go and see Granny."

Through the doors there was a big desk, with loads of nurses behind it chatting. While Mummy spoke to one of them, several of the others crowded around Charlie, ruffling his hair and generally making a fuss. As usual.

The head nurse told Mummy that 'Mrs Whitfield' – that's my Granny's grown-up name – was in a private room at the end of the ward, so we dragged Charlie away from his fan club and off we went.

There were a *lot* of old people. Some were propped up on pillows, smiling; some had visitors, including children who were mostly playing on phones. One old man near the end was snoring like a gruffalo. He had a hairy white chin, crazy, flyaway hair and blue pyjamas with the collar sticking up. Charlie went up to get a better look, because every time he snored his lips wobbled and his head did a little waggle.

Suddenly, he stopped snoring. Completely. He was

totally silent, and very still. Charlie crept closer. "Is he dead?" he said loudly, stepping right up to the bed. He reached out his chubby hand to touch the man's arm.

"Boo!" shouted the man, his eyes flicking open. "I'm not dead yet, little'un! These lovely nurses are keeping me alive," he said, pointing at one of them, who rolled her eyes.

"Ah ha ha!" shouted Charlie. Instead of being frightened like me, he found it funny. "Ah ha ha ha ha! He's a funny man! He play tricks!"

Charlie ran to Mummy, who had come back to find us. "I found Jerry!" he said. "Watch, he do tricks!"

"Leave the poor man alone," said Mummy, although the man didn't seem to mind at all; he just winked at Charlie, and closed his eyes.

We found Granny in a room at the end of the ward.

"What are you doing in here, Granny?" I asked. "Don't you like the other people?"

"It's not that, dear," said Granny, who was sat up in bed. "The nurses just thought I could do with a bit more rest, that's all."

"And you get your own telly," I pointed out, though it was switched off. Boring.

Charlie started to explore the room, though there wasn't much to explore. Just a couple of armchairs and a table on this side of the bed. He disappeared around the other side.

"Where's that cheeky brother of yours gone?" said Granny, but she didn't have to wait long for an answer because suddenly there was a whining, clicking noise and Granny's bed started to lift up into the air.

"Charlie," she said calmly, "you shouldn't be playing with those buttons," as she went higher and higher.

"Sorry," said a voice from under the bed, and the whining noise stopped. Then it started again, and Granny's bed started to sink down.

"Charlie!" said Mummy sharply.

"But I was just putting it back!" he protested, his head popping up into sight. Mummy couldn't argue with that.

Just then, one of the nurses put her head around the door.

"Have you chosen your lunch yet Mrs W?" she asked.

"No, not yet, dear," said Granny. "I was just playing with my grandson. Give me a minute."

"Aah, bless. He looks like a right cutie," said the nurse. "I'll come back in a minute then."

"What's she talking about?" I asked.

"This," said Granny, holding out a piece of paper. "It's how we choose our meals. You tell me what's on the menu, Harriet."

I read it out. "For starters you can have carrot soup..."

"Yuck!" shouted Charlie from under the bed.

"...or a melon boat," I continued. "A melon boat? Weird. What's that?"

"Melon yuck boat cool," said Charlie, who was now peering into Mummy's handbag.

"It's nowhere near as exciting as it sounds, dear," said Granny. "Like most of the food here, I'm afraid. I can't wait to get home."

"There's cottage pie or cauliflower cheese after that," I read, "and then treacle sponge and custard for pudding."

"Cottages yuck flowers yuck custard yuck," muttered Charlie into Mummy's bag. We ignored him.

"Tick the melon and the cottage pie for me please Harriet," said Granny, "and then Charlie, can I trust you to take it to a nurse for me?"

"Yay!" said Charlie, who loves being given jobs to do. He hopped from one foot to the other in excitement while I ticked the boxes and carefully wrote "Mrs

Witfeeld" on the top. Charlie grabbed the menu, and disappeared out of the door.

While he was gone, I told Granny about school, Mummy told her that Charlie still wasn't out of nappies yet, and Granny said he was a bit old for that now, and maybe Mummy should be a bit more strict. I said I thought that was a good idea, too.

After we'd been talking for ages, Mummy asked me to go and find Charlie. Back out on the ward, I couldn't see him anywhere.

"Can I help you?" said a smiley nurse behind the desk.

"I'm looking for my brother," I said. "Mummy sent him with the lunch menu but he hasn't come back."

"Is he the cute little chappy with the curly hair?" she asked.

"He's definitely not cute, but he's certainly curly, so that's probably him," I said.

"In that case, I have a good idea where he might be," she said, and she took me by the hand and we walked down the ward. Everyone was looking at me and smiling. I think I want to be a nurse when I grow up.

"He brought us the menu, but he'd made a few changes," she said, pulling a menu slip out of her pocket and handing it to me.

It was the same menu, but my tick marks had been scribbled out. And in the space next to them, Charlie had drawn a wobbly picture of a green triple-decker burger, and some green chips to go with it.

I turned to the nurse. "My brother is so dumb," I said. "Now Granny will miss her lunch!"

"Don't worry, I've sorted it," said the nurse. "No harm done. Now then, he definitely toddled off this way... but he might just have turned in *here*," she said, pointing at a door with a sign on it: *TV Room.*

"Let's see, shall we?" she said, and pushed open the door.

The room was full of high-backed pink chairs, all turned to face the TV in the opposite corner. *Tree Fu Tom* was on, doing his dance. You could see a few tufts of white hair over the tops of the chairs, so I knew there were people watching, but there was something else, too: the sound of chuntering.

Do you know what chuntering is? It's what Charlie does when he's complaining about something he wants but he can't have. There's lots of things he wants but he can't have, so he does a lot of chuntering: when he asks for a ham and jelly baby sandwich, or a cloud for his birthday, or a gingerbread man instead of his teddy at bedtime.

But this chuntering was the sound of unhappy grown-ups.

"What's going on here then Grace?" my friendly nurse asked the wrinkly old lady who was sitting in the chair nearest the door.

"I think there's something wrong with the telly," she said, winking at me.

"Get it off!" someone shouted from near the front. "I want Countdown back on!"

"This is a rubbish programme! Someone call a nurse!" said another.

"Where has that little lad gone with the remote control?" said a third.

Ah. I knew what was going on here.

I turned around. I'm an expert Charlie-spotter now. I just think, 'Where would Charlie hide?' and I'm usually right. In this case I could see a low wall next to an emergency exit, and chairs pushed up against it.

"Shh," I said to the nurse. "Follow me."

The nurse started to do that funny tiptoe walk that they always do on Scooby-Doo whenever they want to be really quiet. I've never seen a grown-up do that before.

So the nurse and I crept around the back of the chairs, crouched down, and slowly put our heads around the partition.

There, in the small space behind the chair but with a brilliant view of the telly, sat Charlie. But you'll never believe this, because he had a friend! Next to him, separated only by a huge bag of crisps and the remote control, sat the old man in the blue pyjamas. Both of them were pushing big handfuls into their mouths, with bits dropping off everywhere.

The old man saw us. "Looks like we've been rumbled, Charlie boy," he said with a smile.

"Mr Jamieson," said the nurse calmly, "I hate to interrupt your tea party, but this little chap is wanted by his mother. And you're not supposed to be out of bed, either."

"What do you think, Charlie?" he asked. "Shall we give ourselves up?"

Charlie looked at Mr Jamieson and nodded. "They got us," he said. He picked up the crisps and together they crawled out of their hiding place. Charlie sprang to his feet, but Mr Jamieson had to be helped up by the nurse, and it took ages.

"Come on Charlie," said the nurse, taking his hand. But Charlie shook it off, and took the old man's hand instead. Carefully and slowly, Charlie led him back across the room, threading his way between the chairs, ignoring all the chuntering grown-ups. The nurse and I followed.

As they reached the door, the nurse held out her hand. "Umm Charlie, haven't you forgotten something?"

Charlie gave the old man his crisps for safe keeping, and pulled the remote control out of his trousers. He handed it back to the nurse without a word.

"Nice try, soldier," said Mr Jamieson. "You can't win 'em all."

"Goodness, what a cheeky boy you are," said the nurse, but she smiled, and opened the door back to the hospital ward.

Just getting started

So what do you think so far? Which was your favourite bit? Maybe it was when Charlie jumped on the luggage at the airport and pretended to be Superman – Granny had a coughing fit when I told her about that.

Or maybe it was the man on the aeroplane who got a mouthful of cheese – I think of him every time I have cheesy pasta.

But here's a secret: I've hardly started. In fact, I haven't even told you the naughtiest stuff he's done. Yesterday, for instance, we went to the Nature Centre. In the monkey enclosure, he somehow managed to unlock...

Uh-oh, I can hear Mummy calling me for lunch. I'm going to have to stop. If you want to hear more then let me know, and I'll write down the terrible stuff that he's done. And I promise to include the story about the monkeys.

You might need help with this from a grown-up, but you can find out more at cheekycharlie.info or on Facebook too at facebook.com/MeetCheekyCharlie.

Bye bye!